For Laura Rennert. —T. S.

For my nephews, George and Noah. —D. T.

STERLING CHILDREN'S BOOKS
New York

An Imprint of Sterling Publishing Co., Inc.
1166 Avenue of the Americas
New York, NY 10036

Text © 2018 Tammi Sauer
Cover and interior illustrations © 2018 Dan Taylor

ISBN 978-1-4549-2098-4

Distributed in Canada by Sterling Publishing
c/o Canadian Manda Group, 664 Annette Street
Toronto, Ontario, M6S 2C8, Canada
Distributed in the United Kingdom by GMC Distribution Services
Castle Place, 166 High Street, Lewes, East Sussex, BN7 1XU, England
Distributed in Australia by NewSouth Books, 45 Beach Street, Coogee, NSW 2034, Australia

For information about custom editions, special sales, and premium and corporate purchases,
please contact Sterling Special Sales at 800-805-5489 or specialsales@sterlingpublishing.com.

Manufactured in China
Lot #:
2 4 6 8 10 9 7 5 3 1
01/18

sterlingpublishing.com

The artwork for this book was created digitally and traditionally.

Cover and interior design by Jo Obarowski

But the Bear Came Back

by Tammi Sauer

illustrated by Dan Taylor

STERLING CHILDREN'S BOOKS
New York

One ordinary day, a bear knocked on my door.

I politely informed him that bears do not belong in houses.

Then I said, "Go home, bear." And that was that.

But the bear came back. This time he brought a friend.

I said, "Go home, bear. And take that flamingo with you."
And that was that.

But the bear came back.
I pretended no one was home.

No one is home.
Really. Especially
if you are a bear.

Apparently,
bears can't read.

I said, "Go home, bear."
And that was that.

But the bear came back.
Again.

And again.

And again.

Things got a little ridiculous.

And
the
bear
didn't
come
back.

He didn't come back on Monday. "Yes!"

Or Tuesday. "Bear-less."

Or Wednesday.

"Bear?
Are you
there?"

He didn't come back on Thursday.

Or Friday.

Or Saturday.

As for Sunday?

There was no bear anywhere.

"This is unbearable!" I cried.
I missed that bear.
And that was that.

I organized a search party.

REWARD

missing
bear

I tacked up posters.

I set out a bowl of berries.

Then I waited.

And waited.

And waited.

I didn't think he'd *ever* come back.

Then I found my bear. He came back!

I said, "Welcome home, bear."

And that was that.